Margaret Mahy has published over 200 books and is acknowledged all over the world as one of the outstanding children's writers of today. Twice winner of the Carnegie Medal, several of her books have become modern classics. Her books include *Dashing Dog*, illustrated by Sarah Garland, and *Down the Back of the Chair*, also illustrated by Polly Dunbar. In 2006 Margaret was awarded the Hans Christian Andersen Medal for her outstanding contribution to children's literature.

Polly Dunbar was born in Stratford Upon Avon. She started illustrating when she was 16 and has a degree in illustration from the University of Brighton. Her books include *Looking After Louis* and *Measuring Angels*, both written by Lesley Ely, and *Down the Back of the Chair*, also written by Margaret Mahy.

For Harry & Elsie - natural bubblers! - M.M.

For Holly, Craig & Marbles - P.D.

Bubble Trouble copyright © Frances Lincoln Limited 2008
Text copyright © Margaret Mahy 2008
Illustrations copyright © Polly Dunbar 2008

The right of Margaret Mahy to be identified as the Author of this work,
and of Polly Dunbar to be identified as the Illustrator of this work,
has been asserted by them in accordance with the Copyright, Designs and Patents Act, 1988.

First published in Great Britain in 2008 by
Frances Lincoln Children's Books,
4 Torriano Mews, Torriano Avenue, London NW5 2RZ
www.franceslincoln.com

First paperback edition published in 2011

A catalogue record for this book is available from the British Library.

ISBN: 978-1-84780-186-9

Printed in Singapore by Tien Wah Press (Pte) Ltd in January 2011

1 3 5 7 9 8 6 4 2

BUBBLE TROUBLE

Written by

Margaret Mahy

Illustrated by

Polly Dunbar

F

FRANCES LINCOLN
CHILDREN'S BOOKS

LITTLE MABEL blew a bubble and it caused a lot of trouble,

Such a lot of bubble trouble in a bibble-bobble way,

For it broke away from Mabel as it bobbed across the table,

Where it bobbled over Baby, and it wafted him away.

The baby didn't quibble. He began to smile and dribble,
For he liked the wibble-wobble of the bubble in the air.
But Mabel ran for cover as the bubble bobbed above her,
And she shouted out for Mother who was putting up her hair.

At the sudden cry of trouble, Mother took off at the double,

For the squealing left her reeling, made her terrified and tense,

Saw the bubble for a minute, with the baby bobbing in it,

As it bibbled by the letter-box and bobbed across the fence.

In her garden, Chrysta Gribble had begun to cry and cavil

At her lazy brother, Greville, reading novels in his bed.

But she bellowed,
"Gracious, Greville!"
and she grovelled on the gravel,

When the baby in the bubble
bibble-bobbled overhead.

In a garden folly, Tybal, and his jolly mother, Sybil,
Sat and played a game of Scrabble, shouting shrilly as they scored.
But they both began to babble and to scrobble with the Scrabble
As the baby in the bubble bibble-bobbled by the board.

Then crabby Mr Copple and his wife (a carping couple),
Set out arm in arm to hobble and to squabble down the lane.
But the baby in the bubble turned their hobble to a joggle
As they raced away like rockets – and they've never limped again.

Even feeble Mrs Threeble in a muddle with her needle
(Matching pink and purple patches for a pretty patchwork quilt),
When her older sister told her, tossed the quilt across her shoulder,
As she set off at a totter in her tattered tartan kilt.

At the shops a busy rabble met to gossip and to gabble,

Started gibbering and goggling as the bubble bobbled by.

Mother, hand in hand with Mabel, flew as fast as she was able,

Full of trouble lest the bubble burst or vanish in the sky.

After them came Greville Gribble in his nightshirt with his novel

(All about a haunted hovel) held up high above his head,

Followed by his sister, Chrysta (though her boots had made a blister),

Then came Tybal, pulling Sybil, with the Scrabble for a sled.

After them the Copple couple came cavorting at the double,

Then a jogger (quite a slogger) joined the crowd who called and coughed.

Up above the puzzled people – up towards the chapel steeple –

Rose the bubble (with the baby) slowly lifting up aloft.

There was such a flum-a-diddle (Mabel huddled in the middle),
Canon Dapple left the chapel, followed by the chapel choir.
And the treble singer, Abel, threw an apple core at Mabel,

As the baby in the bubble bobbled up a little higher.

Oh, they giggled and they goggled until all their brains were boggled,

As the baby in the bubble rose above the little town.

"With the problem let us grapple," murmured kindly Canon Dapple.

"And the problem we must grapple with is bringing Baby down."

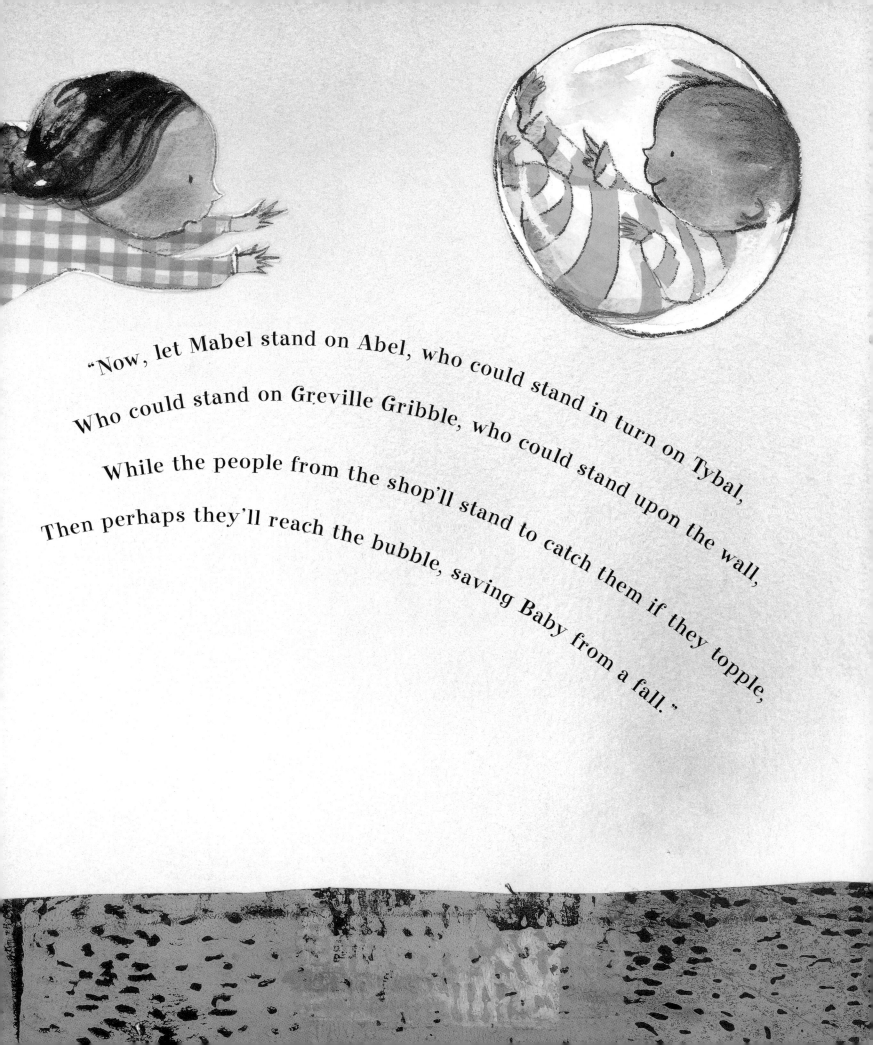

"Now, let Mabel stand on Abel, who could stand in turn on Tybal,

Who could stand on Greville Gribble, who could stand upon the wall,

While the people from the shop'll stand to catch them if they topple,

Then perhaps they'll reach the bubble, saving Baby from a fall."

But Abel, though a treble, was a rascal and a rebel,

Fond of getting into trouble when he didn't have to sing.

Pushing quickly through the people, Abel clambered up the steeple

With nefarious intentions and a pebble in his sling!

Abel quietly aimed the pebble past the steeple of the chapel,
At the baby in the bubble wibble-wobbling way up there.
And the pebble burst the bubble! So the future seemed to fizzle
For the baby boy who grizzled as he tumbled through the air.

What a moment for a mother as her infant plunged above her!

There were groans and gasps and gargles from the horror-stricken crowd.

Sybil said, "Upon my honour, there's a baby who's a goner!"
And Chrysta hissed with emphasis, "It shouldn't be allowed!"

But Mabel, Tybal, Greville and the jogger (christened Neville)

Didn't quiver, didn't quaver, didn't drivel, shrivel, wilt.

But as one they made a swivel, and with action (firm but civil),

They divested Mrs Threeble of her pretty patchwork quilt.

Oh, what calculated catchwork! Baby bounced into the patchwork,

Where his grizzles turned to giggles and to wriggles of delight!

And the people stared dumbfounded as he bobbled and rebounded,

Till the baby boy was grounded and his mother held him tight.

And the people there still prattle – there is lots of tittle-tattle –

For the glory in the story, young and old folk, gold and grey,

Of how wicked treble Abel tripled trouble with his pebble,

But how Mabel (and some others) saved her brother and the day.

MORE TITLES FROM FRANCES LINCOLN CHILDREN'S BOOKS

Down the Back of the Chair
Margaret Mahy
Illustrated by Polly Dunbar

When Dad loses his keys, toddler Mary suspects they are
down the back of the chair.
Join in the fun as the family search and find everything
from a bandicoot and a bumblebee to a string of pearls
and a lion with curls. But will it be enough to save
the family from rack and ruin?

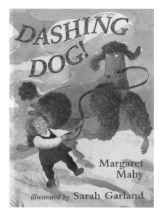

Dashing Dog!
Margaret Mahy
Illustrated by Sarah Garland

Follow the chaotic antics of the dashing dog and his
family in a mad, dizzy and joyful walk along the beach.
With Margaret Mahy's wildly funny sense of humour
and Sarah Garland's exuberant illustrations, this is
a picture book made in heaven!

Measuring Angels
Lesley Ely
Illustrated by Polly Dunbar

When two little girls are given a sunflower seed, they argue
and the little plant grows very badly. "That sunflower is not
happy," says the teacher. So the children decide to make an
angel to help the plant grow. A friendship
develops between the two girls and, as they grow to like each
other, the little plant grows bigger and bigger. . .

Frances Lincoln titles are available from all good bookshops.
You can also buy books and find out more about your favourite titles,
authors and illustrators on our website: www.franceslincoln.com